KEEP ON SINGING

A Ballad of Marian Anderson

by Myra Cohn Livingston

illustrated by Samuel Byrd

Holiday House/New York

Born in Philadelphia—
Her mother told her true,
Whatever you are doing,
Someone's watching you.

Marian earned pennies
Scrubbing people's stairs,
Worked to free her mother
From poverty and cares.

Started in with singing
When she was only three.
Learned the notes and all the parts
And how the words should be.

Joined the Baptist Choir.
Sang most every place.
Learned soprano, alto, tenor,
Even learned the bass.

Heard about a music school,
Thought she would apply.
Girl kept helping others.
Always passed her by.

Marian stood and waited
Till everyone had gone.
We don't take colored, said the girl,
So Marian went on.

Church helped raise some money
To carry on her dream.
Took some formal lessons
Once she turned fifteen.

When she sang *Deep River,*
One teacher wondered why
A tall, calm girl at twilight
Should make him want to cry.

Won a singing contest.
Sang in New York City.
Wonderful, some people said,
But isn't it a pity

We can't book her everywhere—
What a lovely voice.
Too bad she's a Negro,
She can't be our choice.

Marian sang in Europe,
Sang against her fears.
A voice, a great conductor said,
Heard once in a hundred years.

Came back to America,
Her music studies done,

She had sung for kings and queens,
She had overcome.

When she sang in concert halls
Crowds were turned away.
Still hotels and restaurants
Wouldn't let her stay.

Toured in sixty cities,
Often met Jim Crow.
Always prayed *all-seeing God*
Would show her where to go.

Loved to sing the spirituals,
Music, Marian wrote,
That shows *simplicity and faith,*
Humility and hope.

Some of us remember
Constitution Hall
Where she was told she couldn't sing.
Some of us recall

An Easter Sunday long ago
When she stood up to fears
In front of Lincoln's Monument
And eyes were wet with tears.

Marian remembered
Far as the eye could see,
A great wave of good will poured out . . .
Almost engulfing me

Some of us remember,
And we can hear her yet,
The first black woman singer
Invited to the Met.

I may have dreamed of such things
But never thought I'd be
A symbol for young singers
Who follow after me.

Born in Philadelphia,
Her mother told her true.
Whatever you are doing,
Someone's watching you.

Author's Notes on Marian Anderson

1. All italicized words are from Marian Anderson's autobiography, *My Lord, What a Morning*.

2. In *My Lord, What a Morning,* Marian Anderson wrote of her grandmother who "liked to remind people that she was part Indian," while her grandfather "referred to himself as a Black Jew."

3. Marian Anderson claimed she was born on February 27, 1908. When she died in April 1993, the *New York Times* gave the birthdate of February 17, 1902, noting that she celebrated her seventy-fifth birthday on February 17, 1977. A family member found a birth certificate with the date of February 27, 1897. If this is true, she lived to be ninety-six; if the date of 1908 is correct, she lived to be eighty-five. This presents a problem in dealing with her younger years. She may have been seventeen, twenty-three, or twenty-eight when she won the singing contest that took her to Lewisohn Stadium on August 26, 1925.

4. Giuseppi Boghetti was the teacher who professed tears. Before that, she studied with Mary Patterson and Agnes Reifsnyder.

5. The conductor who said her voice was "heard once in a hundred years" was Arturo Toscanini, who made the comment in 1939 in Salzburg, Austria.

6. The term "Jim Crow" dates from the 1880s, when racial segregation became law in many parts of the United States. Jim Crow laws required the separation of races in many public places. During the 1960s the Supreme Court and Civil Rights Acts declared Jim Crow laws invalid.

7. Refused the use of Constitution Hall, Marian Anderson sang in an outdoor concert in front of the Lincoln Memorial on Easter Sunday, April 9, 1939.

8. Marian Anderson sang the role of Ulrica in *Un Ballo in Maschera* (The Masked Ball) at the Metropolitan Opera House on January 7, 1955.

9. The title for this book has been chosen from an album released in 1965 by RCA Red Seal Records, "Jus' Keep on Singin'," featuring Marian Anderson and the Hall Johnson Choir.

Printed in the United States of America
FIRST EDITION
Library of Congress Cataloging-in-Publication Data
Livingston, Myra Cohn.
Keep on singing : a ballad of Marian Anderson / by Myra Cohn Livingston ; illustrated by Samuel Byrd. — 1st ed.
p. cm.
ISBN 0-8234-1098-6
1. Anderson, Marian, 1897–1993 — Juvenile poetry. 2. Afro-American singers — Juvenile poetry. 3. Children's poetry, American.
[1. Anderson, Marian, 1897–1993 — Poetry. 2. Afro-Americans — Poetry. 3. Narrative poetry. 4. American poetry.] I. Byrd, Samuel, ill. II. Title.
PS3562.I945M37 1994 93-46909 CIP AC
811'.54 — dc20